First edition

Published by Ladybird Books Ltd Loughborough Leicestershire UK

© 1992 The Walt Disney Company
Printed in England (3)

DISNEY

WINNIE THE POOH
and the blustery day

Ladybird Books

Christopher Robin and Pooh

In the middle of the Forest, where grown-ups never go, there is a special, enchanted place called the Hundred Acre Wood. This is where a young boy, Christopher Robin, lives with his very best friend, Winnie the Pooh, sometimes called Pooh Bear or just Pooh for short.

Christopher Robin and Pooh have lots of other friends, too. There's Piglet, Kanga and Baby Roo, Tigger, Eeyore the donkey, Rabbit and Owl. They all have happy times together, as well as some very remarkable adventures.

The adventure you're going to hear about now began on a day that started out like any other – but soon turned into a most Extraordinary Day!

One morning, Winnie the Pooh woke up to the sound of the wind howling round his house. He got out of bed and threw open a window.

"Hmm," he said. "I think I'll take a stroll to my Thoughtful Spot and have a Good Think."

On his way, Pooh made up a little hum, and it hummed something like this:

"Hum, dum, dum de de dum,
Hum, dum, dum.
Oh, the wind is lashing lustily,
The trees are thrashing thrustily,
The leaves are rustling gustily,
So it's rather safe to say
That it seems it may turn out to be...
It feels that it will undoubtedly...
It looks like a rather Blustery Day!"

Fortunately, Pooh's Thoughtful Spot was in a sheltered place, well out of the wind. He sat down on a log and tried hard to think of something.

"Think, think, think," said Winnie the Pooh, tapping his head.

Suddenly there was a rumbling at Pooh's feet, and Gopher's head appeared from out of an underground tunnel.

"Say, Sonny," said Gopher when he observed Pooh tapping his head, "do you have a headache?"

"No," replied Pooh. "I was just thinking."

"Well, if I were you," said Gopher, "I'd think about getting out of here as soon as possible."

"Why?" asked Pooh.

"Why?" repeated Gopher. "Because it's Windsday, that's why." And with these words he disappeared again down his burrow.

"Windsday?" said Pooh. "Well, in that case I shall wish everyone a Happy Windsday. And I shall begin with my very dear friend, Piglet."

Pooh Visits Piglet

Piglet lived in a grand old house in a beech tree, with a sign in front that said "TRESPASSERS WILL".

Piglet said that was short for Trespassers William, which had been his grandfather's name. The house had been in the family for a long time, and Piglet was very proud of it.

That particular Blustery Morning, Piglet was outside his house sweeping up the leaves that were swirling round his front door.

Pooh waved to his little friend. "Happy Windsday, Piglet," he said cheerfully.

"Thank you, Pooh," said Piglet. All at once a gust of wind caught him. "But it isn't very happy for me!" he called, as he was swept high into the air.

"Pooh, help!" cried Piglet.

"Don't worry, I'll save you," shouted Pooh, reaching up to catch his friend. But all he caught was the end of Piglet's scarf, and that unravelled like a ball of string.

"Don't let go, Piglet," cried Pooh.

Just then, Kanga and Baby Roo came by. "Look, Mama, look!" said Roo. "A kite!"

"Oh goodness," said Kanga. "That's not a kite – it's Piglet!"

Roo clapped his hands in excitement. "Can I fly Piglet next?" he asked.

But Pooh was too busy to answer. He dug his heels into the ground and held tightly to his end of the wool. Piglet clung to his end, too, but the wind just blew harder, lifting him higher and higher.

Just as Pooh gave the wool another tug, an especially strong gust of wind came along. It blew Pooh right off the ground and carried him along with Piglet.

At last Pooh and Piglet landed in a tree top. Fortunately, it happened to be the tree top where Owl had his house.

Owl was delighted to see his friends' faces pressed against his window. "Pooh and Piglet!" he cried. "This *is* a surprise!

Do come in and make yourselves comfortable." He opened the window, and they blew in.

"Happy Windsday, Owl!" said Pooh.

"Happy Windsday to you, too," said Owl. "It *does* seem to be a rather Blustery Day outside."

"A very, *very* Blustery Day," said Piglet.

"Still," said Owl, "this is just a mild breeze compared with the winter of '67 – or was it '76 – when my Aunt Clara was caught in a *terrible* gale. The wind was so fierce then that..." And Owl went on and on, talking about his relations, so that nobody realised that his house had begun to shake.

Backwards and forwards the house shook and swayed. Then, with one tremendous gust of wind, it came crashing to the ground.

Luckily, no one was hurt. But the house was a terrible mess.

Eeyore Makes a Promise

As soon as Christopher Robin heard of the disaster, he came hurrying along to the scene of Owl's misfortune.

"What a pity!" said Christopher Robin, surveying the damage. "I don't think we'll be able to repair this."

"If you ask me," said Eeyore, "when a house looks like this, it's time to find a new one."

"What a good idea!" said Christopher Robin.

"Leave it to me," said Eeyore. "It might take a day or two, but I'll find a new house for Owl." And he turned and trudged off into the Hundred Acre Wood.

"Thank you, Eeyore," said Owl. "In the meantime, I can tell you all about my Uncle Clyde. He was a very independent barn owl, who didn't give a hoot for tradition. He fell in love with a cat and went to sea in a beautiful pea-green boat! In fact..."

Pooh and Piglet sat listening to Owl's stories until it got dark, when they decided to go home. Owl, of course, no longer had a home, so he had to sleep in the branch of a tree.

The Stormy Night

The Blustery Day turned into a Stormy Night. For Pooh it was a very anxious sort of night, filled with anxious sorts of noises such as he'd never heard before.

"Is that you, Piglet?" Pooh called nervously.

GRRROWL! came the reply.

"Owl, are you out there?"

GRRROWL!

Now, Pooh was not the bravest of bears. He didn't like the new sound one bit – it seemed much too fierce. "I hope it's not Hostile Animals," he said to himself.

He tried calling out one more time. "Come in, Christopher Robin."

But the answer was still the same – GRRROWL!

Pooh hid his head under the bedclothes.

Suddenly there came a loud knocking at the door. Pooh, being a Bear of Very Little Brain, decided to invite the new sound in. He picked up his popgun, crept to the door and slowly opened it...

Pooh Meets Tigger

WHOOSH!

In bounced a stripey creature, who knocked Pooh off his feet.

"Hello! I'm Tigger!" said the strange animal.

"Goodness!" gasped Pooh. "You scared me."

"Of course I did. Everyone's scared of Tiggers. Who are you?"

"I'm Pooh," said Pooh.

"What's a Pooh?" asked Tigger, bouncing on Pooh's stomach.

"You're sitting on one," said Pooh.

"Sorry," said Tigger, bouncing off.

Suddenly Tigger spotted a strange-looking creature in Pooh's mirror.

"Who's that?" he asked.

"It looks like another Tigger to me," said Pooh.

"Nonsense!" said Tigger. "I'm the only Tigger." He pulled a fierce face. "Just watch me scare the stripes off this imposter!"

But the other animal seemed to pull an even fiercer face. Tigger was terrified, and he hid under the table.

Pooh offered Tigger some honey to make him feel better, but Tigger didn't seem to like honey.

"Yuk!" he said. "This icky, sticky stuff is only fit for Heffalumps and Woozles!"

Pooh had never heard of Heffalumps and Woozles.

"What do they do?" he asked Tigger.

"Nothing much – just steal honey!" cried Tigger, bouncing right out of Pooh's front door.

Pooh could hardly believe his ears. If what Tigger had said about Heffalumps and Woozles was true, he would have to protect his honey. He picked up his popgun and began to march.

"March, march, march," he said, standing as straight and tall as he could.

Suddenly he caught sight of another bear carrying a popgun, marching straight towards him.

"Oh! Hello!" said Pooh.

The other bear didn't answer.

"Am I glad to see you!" Pooh went on. "It's much more friendly with two. Now, you march that way and I'll go this way."

Pooh was so jittery he didn't realise he was talking to his own reflection in the mirror. He just went on marching, hour after hour after hour. At last, when he was too tired to stand up any longer, he flopped down exhausted.

The Dream

While the wind blew and the rain came down outside, Winnie the Pooh sat beside his honey pots, fast asleep. And while he slept, he dreamt a very peculiar dream. It was all about Horrible Heffalumps and Wild Woozles.

Pooh dreamt of
giant honey pots
coming to warn him
about the Heffalumps
and Woozles.

"Beware, beware,
they're everywhere!"
chanted the honey pots,
whirling round Pooh.

Pooh began to feel
quite dizzy. But still
the honey pots sang
their warning:
"Heffalumps and
Woozles steal honey!"

Now, Pooh had no
idea what Heffalumps
and Woozles actually
looked like, but in his
dream they were
terrifying. Some of the
Woozles looked like
huge jack-in-the-boxes
with big noses. They
stuck out their tongues
and laughed at Pooh.

Others were in the
shape of giant
balloons.

The Heffalumps came in all shapes and sizes. One was like a giant bumblebee with an elephant's head and feet. It chased Pooh and buzzed round his head, trying to grab his precious honey. Then a huge watering can overturned above Pooh. Pooh tried to escape, but he just got wetter, until...

...he woke with a start – and saw that the water was real! It had rained all night, and Pooh's house was filled with puddles.

Of course, the first thing that Pooh did was to try to rescue his honey. But he got his head stuck in one of his honey pots, and he went floating helplessly out into the Forest, his legs waving in the air.

The rain had got into Piglet's house too, and Piglet woke to find himself in

the midst of a flood. His bed and all his furniture were floating away, and the water was still rising!

Piglet didn't know what to do, but he knew he needed help. So he found some paper and wrote a note that said:

He put the note into a bottle and threw the bottle into the water.

The water carried the bottle out of the house and away into the Forest. And soon the water carried Piglet away, too.

The Rescue of Piglet

By morning, nearly all of the Hundred Acre Wood was flooded. But the water didn't quite reach Christopher Robin's house, so that was where everyone gathered to shelter from the storm.

Everyone, that is, except Eeyore. He stubbornly refused to stop searching for a new house for Owl.

Meanwhile, Baby Roo had made an Important Discovery. "Look!" he cried. "I've found a bottle. And there's a message inside!"

Christopher Robin took out the note and read it.

"We have to rescue Piglet right away!" said Christopher Robin. "Owl, you go and find him and tell him we're coming."

Owl set off at once, and he soon saw two tiny objects below him. As he flew

closer, he saw that the objects were
Pooh hanging on to a chair, and Piglet,
spinning in a whirlpool in one of Pooh's
honey pots.

"Don't worry, you two!" called Owl.
"Help is on the way!"

A Hero's Party

Before long, Pooh, Owl and Piglet had drifted all the way to Christopher Robin's house.

Christopher Robin was overjoyed to see Pooh. Then he saw that Piglet was safe and sound in Pooh's honey pot. "Pooh, you've rescued Piglet!" cried Christopher Robin. "You're a Hero!"

"I am?" said Pooh, a little uncertainly.

"Yes," said Christopher Robin. "And as soon as the flood is over I shall give you a Hero's Party."

And so, when at last the Hundred Acre Wood had dried out, Christopher Robin gave Pooh his Hero's Party.

In the middle of all the excitement, Eeyore appeared and made an announcement.

"I've found it," he said.

"Found what, Eeyore?" asked Christopher Robin.

"Owl's new house," replied Eeyore.

Owl's New House

Everyone followed Eeyore through the Forest, eager to see what he had found. Much to their surprise, he stopped right in front of Piglet's house.

"Er… why have we stopped here, Eeyore?" asked Christopher Robin.

"This is it," said Eeyore. "Owl's new house. It even has Owl's name in front – W O L."

"So it does," said Owl, delighted.

"Well done, Eeyore! It's an excellent house. Don't you think so, everyone?"

"It's a very nice house indeed," said Christopher Robin. "The only thing, Eeyore, is that it's – "

"It's the best house in the world," Piglet blurted out. "And it's just the right house for our good friend Owl. I hope he'll be very happy in it."

No one but Pooh noticed the tiny tear that rolled down Piglet's cheek.

"But Piglet," said Christopher Robin, "where will *you* live now?"

"I guess I shall live..." Piglet began, "I suppose I shall live..."

"He'll come and live with me!" said Pooh. "Won't you, Piglet?"

"Why... why, yes, Pooh!" said Piglet happily. "Thank you! I should love to!"

"Now we have *two* heroes!" said Christopher Robin. "Pooh is a hero for saving Piglet, and Piglet is a hero for giving his house to Owl. So let's make our One Hero Party a *Two* Hero Party!''

Everyone thought that was a Splendid Idea. Christopher Robin got his drum and led everyone in a joyful parade back to his house.

It was a wonderful party, with games to play and good things to eat and drink. There were extra pots of honey for Pooh, and four big helpings of haycorns for Piglet.

There wasn't another Blustery Day in the Hundred Acre Wood for a long time, but Christopher Robin, Winnie the Pooh and their friends had many more adventures that you can read about.

Grown-ups think that all these stories are make-believe, and that Christopher Robin's friends are just stuffed toys. But you and I know better, don't we?

Of course we do – as sure as there's a Hundred Acre Wood!